I was happy with my life. And who wouldn't be?
Beautiful women, money, a job that I could sleep through
and still make bank. But I was bored. And I never could
walk away from a challenge.

This challenge turned out to be brunette. Feisty. Just the
way I like them. But innocent. Too innocent for me. Too
innocent to do anything other than sample and toss back.
Anything more would be too risky, too much work.

I was unprepared for Julia Campbell. I should have done
my homework, should have looked before diving into
unfamiliar waters. Ditching her proved to be problematic,
my sexual needs greater than my common sense.

She was different. She became more than a challenge.

She may just bring my world crashing down.

This novella is a companion piece to Blindfolded
Innocence, a #1 Erotica Bestseller, which is available
wherever books are sold.

the block

Brad De Luca sat across from Kent Broward and Hugo Clarke, the large conference room crowded with tension in the well-appointed room. It was how meetings between them always were, and why they restricted this pain to quarterly events.

They had discussed the financial statements, upcoming cases, and a litigation that had been filed against the firm. Now there was only one item left, and he glanced at his watch impatiently. It was already seven o'clock.

"Okay," Clarke said, sliding a slim stack of folders before him. "Interns. We have twelve coming this semester."

Both men turned to Brad expectantly, and he groaned, leaning back in his chair with a cocky smile. "I know. No fucking the interns."

Kent Broward winced, the word unpleasant to his ears. "It's not a joking matter. You opened our firm to serious liability when you did that—"

Brad interrupted, shooting him a look that silenced his next sentence, "We open ourselves up to liability every time we take on a case. Don't preach to me about liability."

The third man leaned forward. "Kent, Brad understands the situation. It's not going to happen again."

Brad gave the silver-haired man a steely look, his jaw tight, and reached across the table, flipping the top folder open and looking at the file. It was bullshit that they still went through this, at every quarterly meeting, at every opportunity that an intern was mentioned. It was three years ago, and the girl had all but spread her legs on his desk and forced his cock inside.

He stared at the first folder.

A slim Asian girl, the type who would shrink every time he raised his voice, stared out at him, paper-clipped to an impressive resume which indicated her complete lack of social life. He tossed it aside.

A black kid with glasses, who had an interest in criminology.
A redheaded girl with sunburnt skin and braces, 'crocheting' on her list of activities.

A blond kid, perfect features with a side of preppy, his personality visible through the cocky grin he flashed the photographer.

Another Asian, this one male, whose serious expression alone depressed the hell outta Brad.

He flipped through five more folders, his brain counting as he went. All intelligent. All impressive. All uninteresting. He reached the last one and looked up.

"Where are the rest?"

Clarke cleared his throat. "Kent and I already selected our candidates."

"That's bullshit. Let me see their files." He held out a hand, a pointless exercise since neither man had a green folder in their slim stack.

"We don't have the files here. We chose them yesterday. It's done. Choose yours." Kent shot him a bored look, one that barely masked disgust.

"We've never done it that way before," Brad said evenly, looking at Clarke.

"It's an intern, Brad. You've barely given two thoughts to any you've had in the past … with the one notable exception. Pick one and let's move on. My wife's got dinner waiting."

He flipped back through the stack, going for the most interesting out of the bunch—the blond with the cocky smile—tossing the others back into the center of the table. They would be distributed among the junior partners, each bookworm going to a proper attorney who'd work their free bones to the quick.

"Fine. Anything else?" he asked brusquely.

"That's all I have. Kent?"

The man shook his head in response. In unison, all of their chairs slid back.

the child

Two weeks later, he pushed open the door to his office and came face-to-face with a kid straight off the pages of J. Crew — short blonde hair, piercing blue eyes, and a jawbone that would be a breeze to crack. Brad stopped, glancing into the lobby and then back at the kid.

"Who are you, and what are you doing in my office?"

His tone made the kid blink, and he fidgeted, moving a black folder from one hand to the other, before tucking it under his arm. "I'm Todd Appleton, sir. I'm your intern."

Oh, right. It was already here. Intern season. "And who told you to come in here?"

"I just assumed … sir. No one told me."

Brad grinned, moving past him and behind the desk. "You got past those three women?" He pointed toward the large lobby desk that housed his secretaries, three women who made a habit of chewing and spitting out little children. "And waltzed in here?"

The kid shifted again, adjusting the collar of his blue shirt that perfectly matched his eyes. "Everyone seemed to be in a meeting when I came in. This office had your name on it, so—"

Brad waved his hand. "Whatever. Don't come in here again unless I call for you. Rebecca, or one of the other girls, will get you set up in an office. In the meantime, sit down and shut up. You can listen in on my calls."

There was a sharp rap on the door, and he glanced up to see Marilyn step in, a stack of folders in her hand. She moved forward, sending a quick look toward the kid.

Brad gestured with his hand. "Todd, this is Marilyn—she runs this wing, listen to whatever she tells you. Marilyn, Todd will sit in on my calls, please come and get him when Mrs. Washington arrives."

The woman nodded quickly and stepped for the door, shooting the boy a smile that contained more vinegar than sugar.

Brad chuckled, glancing at his desk clock and writing down the time as he dialed a number on his phone.

first sight

Two weeks later.

He saw her speaking to Marilyn, a bit of hair falling over her forehead, catching on her glasses. He stood by the glass wall of his office, his eyes studying her, trying to place her face, her body. The name escaped him, but the hair, the glasses … She worked downstairs, handled travel arrangements. He watched the folder exchange hands, watched her smile and begin to turn. And reaching up, before she stepped outside, he rapped on the glass, gesturing for her when the noise caught her eye.

He finished his call, watching her walk to the door, picking up details as she moved closer. Small waist. Small bust. Huge eyes, shielded behind thick glasses. A confidence to her step despite the tremor in her hands. She was nervous.

He ended the call, his mind working, filing the clues and realizing the possibility of error in identification as he spoke. "I need a car."

She was confused, and the longer she stood there, the more certain he was that she was not the travel girl. She was someone new, someone different. Someone who had somehow escaped his notice. Someone, given her employer, he should avoid.

He watched her walk out, noting the curve of her ass, his cock responding without thought, his hand reaching for the phone, dialing the number before he had good mind to rein it in.

And when he found out who she was, his smile widened with the discovery of the forbidden.

Brad stopped by Rebecca's office, stepping inside and shutting the door.

She looked up from her computer with raised brows, plucked to perfection. "Wow. That didn't take long." She glanced at her watch. "Four and a half hours. Hell, I'm surprised you made it that long."

He stuck his hands in his pockets, glaring at her in a way that would cause most to tremble. "What are you talking about?"

She met his glare head on, her beauty not affected by her two hundred and fifty pound figure. "Cut the bullshit. I know you're here about her."

"Who?"

"Julia she's-an-intern-so-forget-about-her Campbell," she said the name with a smug smile, entirely too happy with herself.

"Who?"

She snorted. "Oh please. Give me one other reason you are in my office with the door closed." She waited expectantly, her brows raised. "Well? Spit it out."

He furrowed his brow, searching for a case name, a menial errand, anything to shut her up, but came up blank. He pulled out a chair and sat down. "Fine. You know me. Now give me the goods."

She pulled open her file cabinet, her fingers deftly dancing over the tabs until she stopped, yanking out a file and holding it to her ample breasts. "What'cha got to offer?"

"Your job," he said pointedly.

She scrunched her mouth to the side and looked at the ceiling. "Nope. You couldn't sharpen a pencil without me here. Something else."

"Is there anything in there I even want?" he drawled out, leaning forward and looking into her eyes.

She leaned forward as well, her mouth curving into a playful smile. "Ohhhh yeah, De Luca. But you already know that or else you wouldn't be darkening my doorstep."

"Fine. A day of PTO."

"Three days," she countered.

"Two," he said with a wry smile. "Though I don't know who will sharpen my pencils during that time. Now *speak.*"

She flipped open the file, a glossy 4x6 staring out from the pages. He inhaled without thought, the brunette beauty devastating with her glasses off and hair down.

"Yep," Rebecca said smugly. "No wonder Broward snatched her up. Word in the halls is that they almost didn't accept her, given her looks, but Broward said he would handle it—keep your paws at bay and her safe and sound."

He frowned, flipping over her photo and picking up the application. Fucking with Broward's intern wasn't the best idea for office politics, not when combined with his rocky past. The right thing, the smart thing, would be to forget he saw her and move on. "Impressive GPA," he remarked, noting her Dean's List standing and numerous accolades. "She a bookworm?"

"More like brilliant," Rebecca said. "Going off her Facebook page, she's got an active social life. So she either lives off no sleep, or doesn't have to work hard for that 4.0."

"A boyfriend?" He looked up from the file to meet her eyes.

"Does it *matter*?" she said, with the voice of a disapproving parent.

"I'm not in here asking about her because I need a new file clerk. Answer the question."

"It isn't in her application," she pointed out.

"Neither are her Facebook status updates." He gave her a hard look.

"Fine. She just ended an engagement," she said flatly. "So she's vulnerable. Not looking for someone to waltz in and fuck with her head."

He shot her a wounded look. "You give me no credit."

"Wrong, Mr. De Luca. When it comes to fucking, I give you all the credit." With that, she snatched the folder away, shutting it and pushing it to the side. "We're good, right? You're going to behave? Keep to this wing and let her keep to hers?"

He regarded her carefully, his eyes unfocused, and pondered the question.

the chase

Thursday: two days later.

He couldn't get away from this girl. She was a vice that followed him around, from her Tuesday appearance in the East Wing to the Wednesday early morning call. A call from his cousin, digging for information on Julia for a man named Bob. A call that had stuck with him, the forbidden fruit becoming more enticing the more he discovered.

Broward's intern, who apparently hid a sexual fire beneath that sweet cardigan. Another man hot on her trail. Calling around, asking questions. *Competition.*

He had gone straight to the office after the call, finding her in the west kitchen, butter on her lips, the scent of fear coming off her skin. But she'd had bite, shrugging off his advances, pushing away despite the attraction that flickered in her eyes.

It was there. Heat between them. And when he had pulled up to her in the garage? Ordered her to get in the car and go to lunch? She had obeyed, as she should have. He was a senior partner, she an intern. She should have wiped drool off her mouth and scampered in, ready to assist him in any way that he deemed necessary.

But she didn't behave. She was unimpressed, sarcastic. Not swooned by Centaur's grandiose entrance or the restaurant's exorbitant prices, she had looked him in the eye when she spoke and called him out on his bullshit. She had been, simply put, fascinating. He wanted more, wanting to know what made her tick, what her story was, if she was a local college slut or the innocent that her flushed cheeks portrayed. And what he really wanted, what he thought about every time she put a piece of meat into her mouth, or sipped the glass of white wine, was putting his hands and cock on every part of her body. Making her quiver, making her grip his skin and scream his name.

And now, the third day of her spell, he was stepping into Kent Broward's wing, glancing at his watch. He had ten minutes, max, before the staff started to arrive. Ten minutes to talk her into a second date.

She wasn't alone in her office, and he stared at the pair, Julia nervous, her gaze flitting from him to the man, then back again. The man also quaked, his hand shaking as it smoothed down the hair on his soon-to-be balding head. This must be the man whom his cousin had called him about. The accountant who was head over heels obsessed with the intern who would soon be Brad's.

What did she see in this weakling? His pressed suit, fresh haircut, and girly scent practically screamed whipped. Maybe she liked that, maybe she wanted to run over her partner, have him scurry around whenever she barked. He met her eyes, seeing the flash in her depths. She had fire. He liked fire.

He spoke, allowing his words to come out as a grumble, the threat in them causing the scrawny man to widen his eyes. "I need to speak to Julia if you are both done here."

There was an awkward goodbye, and then the man was gone, and Brad and Julia were alone in the office. She crossed her arms and stared at him with a look that was meant to be intimidating. "What, pray tell, did you need to speak to me about that just couldn't wait?"

He ignored her question, tilting his head in the direction of the exit, guessing at the answer to his question before he finished speaking. "Who is he?"

"Bob. He is a—"

"I know who he is. I meant who is he to you?"

Her eyes narrowed. "*He* is nothing to me."

"Are you dating?"

"Is that any of your business?"

"It is if he's visiting you at work."

She threw up her hands, turning to her desk. "Oh, please! Don't even pull that card."

He repeated the question, intent on finding the answer. "Are you dating?"

"No."

Her conviction and attitude satisfied him, and he leaned against the doorway, letting his eyes roam, traveling from perfect feet upward, past long legs, a navy dress that hugged the firm outline of her body, before settling on devourable lips, perfect features, flushed cheeks, and eyes that challenged him to make an inappropriate comment. He had the sudden desire to push her back on her desk and claim her body right now. His mouth moved without provocation, words coming out before he could harness them. "Come to Vegas with me this weekend."

"What?" She looked at him like he had three heads. He wanted to ask himself the same question. This was a horrible idea, one that would certainly bite him in the ass.

He rephrased the question, cursing his psyche with every word flowing smoothly off of his traitorous lips. "I'm going to Vegas this weekend. Why don't you come?" He tried for a welcoming tone, but the words came off more as an order.

"Are you serious?"

"Dead serious." And suddenly he was, the desire to rip off that dress and have her naked in his hands too tempting to resist.

She smiled demurely. "I appreciate the offer, but I'll have to pass."

He smiled. "Think it over. I'll have you back safe and sound by Monday."

Those damn arms crossed again, the motion pressing her breasts together and offering them up to him. "I appreciate the offer, but no."

He raised his eyebrows and looked at her, noting the steel in her gaze, the challenge only making her more appealing. "No boyfriend?"

"No."

"Think it over." He flashed a smile at her, the smile that normally weakened women's resolve and had them ready and willing to do whatever he proposed. He turned on one heel, his brain begging for one final look at her, and left, heading back to his domain.

She would come. Now that his brash mouth had issued the invitation, there was no alternative but to make sure she came. Brad De Luca didn't get rejected. Especially not by a twenty-something intern who had probably never been properly fucked in her life.

It was a horrible idea, flying an intern to Vegas. Kent Broward's intern especially. If this came to light, *when* this came to light, there would be hell to pay. But that woman back there, her feisty attitude and tight body ... one night with her could very well be worth the downfall.

The aftermath, when she would turn needy and want more than sex ... the constant calls, persistent emails, those would not be worth it. That would be a headache that his schedule wouldn't have time for. He swallowed, pushing open the double doors to the East Wing, regretting the invitation with every step he took away from her.

the city of sin

52 hours later: Vegas

2:45 AM. Too damn late. He collected a stack of chips and let them fall through his hand, watching them bounce and drop on the green felt.

"Your luck has turned," the heavyset man before him said, gathering the cards. "You should stop for the night."

Brad looked up, shaking his head and sliding a single black chip forward. "Another hand."

He reached for the glass, downing the remaining bit of bitter liquor. It was out of his norm — continuing to play when his luck had turned. But he needed to be down here and out of the suite. In the suite was she … and he didn't know how to handle her.

A waitress materialized at his side, setting another cold glass before him. He nodded, passing her a tip, and tapped on the table, asking for another card. He stared at his hand, trying for the hundredth time to rid his mind of her image.

They had checked in late, heading up to the room first, the bellman putting away their bags. He had expected them to go out, for dinner or drinks, when she had come to pieces, standing in the middle of the suite, her eyes welling with tears, her mouth basically accusing him of bringing her here for sex. It was like she expected him to bend her over the sofa as soon as the door closed behind the bellman.

He swallowed another mouthful of whisky. Her concerns were well-founded. He had assumed they would fuck, but he was in no rush. It wasn't something that needed to happen on this trip. This trip had been intended more for … hell … he didn't know why he had brought her here. The whole damn thing didn't make any sense. All he knew was that look in her eyes — that fragile, terrified expression — told him he needed to be careful. Keep his distance, keep her clothed, untouched. She was not one of the women who lay on his desk and begged for a fucking. She was, apparently, fairly inexperienced. And she would take the sex as more than it was.

Stay away. Keep his distance. An easy decision to make when he sat thirty-two floors below her, alcohol and hours of distraction between them. It might be a different story when he was in her presence again.

He pushed the remaining chips towards the line. "All in. Last hand."

"Good luck," the dealer said with a somber look.

"Thanks. I need it."

His new resolution lasted long enough for him to stumble upstairs, his pockets heavy with winnings, and collapse on the bed in the extra bedroom. He woke five hours later with a headache and sheet imprints on his face. He rolled over, rubbing his face, and sat up, wincing at bright light that poured through the windows.

Jacking off helped, his hand stroking his cock under the hot spray of the shower. He directed his thoughts to Bethany, his latest fuck, thinking about her soft breasts against his body, the slap of them when she rode him to completion. He avoided any thought of the brunette one room over, gritting his teeth as he came, the evidence of his satisfaction washed down the stone walls with the spray of water.

He was proud of himself, of his control, his resolution fully in tact. He walked in the bedroom, wearing boxer briefs, and headed to his suitcase. He stopped, just inside the door, his eyes on her, his feet moving and carrying him to the side of the bed, his hand gently lifting the covers slightly until her face was revealed.

Dark hair cradled a sweet face, impossibly perfect in its features, relaxed and angelic in sleep. No hint of her feisty personality shown. In sleep she looked innocent and untouched. He glanced at the clock, his desire to join her in the bed tempting.

He shouldn't. He should dress and leave her, putting a door or two in between them until she was awake and dressed. But he had never done what he should, the appeal of danger much more interesting. He pulled the sheet back, settling his body over hers, one knee on either side of her body, and leaned forward, pressing his lips to the open skin of her neck. He promised himself that if she stiffened, if she resisted, he would roll off. Stand up. Walk out of this suite and away from this woman.

A moan. The woman moaned, and it was the most carnal sound he had ever heard. Her body shifted beneath him, her pelvis lifting up slightly, and he lowered his body to meet it. He moved his lips to her ear, wanting to reassure her. "This isn't about sex, I promise."

She giggled, her hands startling him when they touched his thighs, sliding up until they reached the cotton of his underwear and she squeezed, his muscles jumping under her touch. He lifted slightly off of her, taking her touch as permission, and ran a gentle hand down her body, trailing the lines of her bra, her skin soft and smooth beneath his fingers, her breath catching as he slid his hand lower, down the slope of her stomach, before marginally sneaking under the lace hem of her panties.

He should stop. He should slide off of her and curl his body around hers. Turn this situation into a sweet, innocent one. But he couldn't. For the same reason that he was lying on top of her right now. He. Couldn't. Stay. Away.

"If this isn't about sex, what are you doing?" she asked softly, making a sound somewhere between a whimper and a moan.

He moved, shifting his body, feeling the heat of hers as their skin brushed. "It's about proving you wrong ... and pleasing you." Three nights earlier, at the office, over pizza and sodas, she had confessed to never having experienced an orgasm. That she couldn't. A ridiculous statement, and one that he intended to disprove.

His fingers continued their sweep, traveling over the tiny material of her panties, running up and down her mound. She moaned and responded immediately, pulling her smooth legs free and wrapping them around his waist. She arched her back, pressing her breasts into him, and he took advantage of the movement, moving his free hand underneath her and firmly grabbing her delicious ass, squeezing it hard, and loving the feel of it in his hands. He had been wanting, dreaming, of this ass, of having it in his hands, bent over before him. She gasped, pushing against him, and he released her, sliding his hand up and gripping her long hair, pulling it until her eyes were staring into his.

They caught the morning light, brown embers burning playfully, her mouth curved into a smile, her eyes dancing over his, a challenge in them. She was so different, so full of fire and fun, a combination of the two, and he couldn't wait to see what happened when those eyes turned carnal.

She thrust up, catching him off guard, and kissed him, her lips confident, pushing past any resistance with one playful swipe of her tongue. He groaned, letting go of all control he'd struggled to maintain, dominating with his mouth until she was flat on the bed beneath him, his arm moving from under her, his body settling atop hers, held up enough by his elbows so as not to crush her.

The kiss was a battle, an initial testing between two warriors, their kiss matching in dips and tastes, until he swept the pieces off the map and claimed her as his own.

He ground against her without thinking, the desire to have her overwhelming his body, his cock anxious for more, wanting the silky feel of her skin, awaiting a release, greedy for more. She froze against his mouth, and he lifted his head, their eyes locking, and he brushed against her one last time.

Her eyes changed when his arousal made contact, taking the journey from shock to vixen, and she pushed, trying to roll him over. He shook his head, and lowered his head and his hips, reclaiming her with his mouth, his body once again tight against hers.

She squirmed, her hands moving, sliding along the ridges of his stomach. Reaching down, feeling for him, her hands almost *there* when he captured them. Holding them still, he slid off of her, moving to lie beside her, one of his big hands pinning both of hers above her head.

His eyes took a greedy and unapologetic tour of her body, his free hand leading the way. He pulled down the top of her bra, allowing her breasts to be free and exposed, pink nipples erect in the morning air. He ran his hand down and over the top of her panties, letting out a measured breath when he felt the wet silk between her legs. His grin grew, and he teased the area through the panties, running his hand back and forth, applying slight pressure on the fabric, and watching the change in her eyes. Then he slipped a finger past the fabric and inside of her.

He had touched hundreds of women, the inside of a woman's body as familiar as his own cock. But the feeling of her, the heat inside, wet and tight, gripping his finger with a sucking pull was unlike any else. He could feel his control ebbing, and it was everything he could do not to roll above her and pull out his cock. The feel of her on his finger … it would be heaven to be inside of her.

"Oh my God, Julia," he breathed. "What am I going to do with you?" It wasn't a hypothetical question. This was bad; this was worse than the other intern, worse than Kent Broward's wife. This girl was a poison that could ruin him. She was innocent, inexperienced, yet burned with fire, curiosity, and challenge. His body was ready for the task, pushing against the starting gate, wanting to fuck her senseless and brand her forever as his own. His mind was backing away with hands up, fear and panic gripping his chest.

The vixen beneath him moved, catching him off guard, distracted by his inner turmoil. She ripped her hands free, her eyes flashing with a combination of lust, anger, and hunger. She tried to move, to climb on top of him, but he easily held her off, pressing down on her shoulders and straddling her with his body.

"I want to suck your dick," she whispered, her voice thick with desire.

He shook his head at me. "This is about you. I want to please you."

"Having your dick in my mouth is what will please me!" she shot back.

He tried to relax his breathing, tried to sound reasonable and in control. "You said you couldn't come."

Her eyes narrowed. "Seriously, let's just drop it. I've accepted it. You need to do the same."

"Do I look like a man who gives in easily?" As his mind screamed obscenities, he forced her back on the bed and moved, skimming down that delicious body until his face was at her stomach.

"Waaa ... stop!" Her voice came out shrill and panicked, causing him to pause and look up.

"What?"

"What are you doing?"

An excellent question. He should be packing his bags and getting the hell out of here. "What do you think I'm doing?"

"I ... err ... don't do that." She sounded nervous, almost anxious.

He ran a finger under the line of her panties, begging for a chance to feel her again, his mouth wanting the taste of her on his tongue. "Don't do that, or haven't done that?"

"Both."

"Julia. Trust me."

Her mouth worked, indecision in her eyes, and then she nodded.

Brad slowly rolled down her panties, his eyes feasting on her skin as it was unveiled. A thin line of hair, cut short, leading to the lips between her legs, her knees stubbornly together, resisting when he pulled them apart. And then she was before him, her eyes large, her body open. And she was the most beautiful thing he had ever seen.

She had come apart underneath his mouth, muscles contracting, her voice breaking, legs trembling, sex throbbing underneath his tongue. It had happened quickly, her body tuned and ready, needy for stimulation that had never been given. He didn't know what her ex-boyfriends had done with her, but they had never taken the time to care for her properly. It had taken every ounce of his willpower to stand when he was done, to step back, to go to the closet and dress. He ran his hand along the hard ridge of his cock, the ache in his balls surprising, given his morning shower. He stuffed it into pants and grinned, thinking of her moans, her peak, the way she had called his name when she came.

He walked back into the room, his eyes trailing over her body, relaxed on the sheets, a lazy smile across her face. And he wondered how he would survive two more days with her. Because fucking her wasn't an option. Not with the roller coaster his mind was on. Not with the risks that waited for them back at the firm. She rolled slightly, her naked body curving, and he felt his cock harden again.

Two days.

Might as well be an eternity.

the path to hell

Twelve hours later.

If the devil had a name, it would be Alexis. She was pure sex, pure temptation, and could get him off within fifteen minutes. And now, he was going straight to hell.

It was necessary. He couldn't be around Julia any longer, not without lying her down and taking what he really wanted. He needed a release, a distraction. Something to remind him who he was and what he liked — both things Alexis knew very well.

He hadn't planned on seeing Alexis this trip. But Julia had challenged him, wanting to see Vegas 'De Luca-style.' And if a strip club experience was what she wanted, then Saffire was the place to go.

Justification was a strong tool. He knew that, knew the path his cock was insistent on him taking. He could have brought her somewhere else — visited a girly martini bar and one of the hot clubs. But instead they were heading down the Strip, toward Saffire, his muscles tightening in anticipation. He texted Alexis, alerting her to their arrival. She would know what to do, how to distract Julia while she handled his needs. And then they could leave, his body drained, his mind free, and he could return to playing the gentleman he wasn't.

The car slowed, rumbling over the gravel, until it came to a stop before Saffire's red doors.

Hell. He had arrived. His cock awoke, thickening in his pants, and he turned to smile at Julia.

He fucked Alexis without mercy, getting his fill, but making sure she was satisfied before pulling out. She dropped to her knees, taking him into her mouth and swallowing every bit of him, her eyes on his. Watching. Analyzing. The orgasm should have released his tension, lulled him into a calm and controlled state, but it didn't work. He was still frustrated, on edge, her body not fulfilling him in the way that it normally did, his mind still wound tightly.

And Alexis picked up on it. "You've never fucked me like that before."

"Sure I have." He zipped up his pants, avoiding her critical eyes.

"No, not that ... hungry. Is it from being around her?"

He teased one of her nipples. "You sound a little jealous."

She slapped his hand away. "I don't care about you enough to be jealous. I just don't know why you're wasting your time with that lily-white baby when we both know what you need. And it ain't her."

Brad watched her, the line of her muscles, the length of her hair. She was exactly like most of the women he fucked. And nothing like Julia.

Alexis was right. What he needed was a woman who knew her sexuality. Who was open and forthcoming about what she wanted and from whom she would get it. He needed a woman who thought nothing of sucking his cock outside a restaurant, one who was confident enough to share him with another woman. That was what he — or rather, his body — needed.

His mind wanted something else entirely. Someone he could take to functions, wine and dine, engage in meaningful conversation with. Someone who would accept him despite his last name and the skeletons in his closet.

The problem was that they were colliding ideals, qualities that would never be in the same woman. And neither matched Julia. Not the sexual willingness, or the life partner. She was too pure for him, too young. She would take one look at the real Brad and take off for parts unknown.

Alexis tilted her head back and blew a ring into the dark room. "Does she know where you are right now?"

"No. I assume you told Montana to keep her busy." That was probably going to be a problem. He would have to tell her—deception not part of this game. How she reacted would be telling. But even if she ran—even if she went crazy and cursed him to eternity—it would be better than if he had weakened and slept with her.

If he had fucked her, laid her down and ran his cock over her body? Pressed against her sweet pussy and pushed deeper with his cock? Felt that hot bundle of muscles squeeze and tighten, slow thrusting inside of her until they both came? It would have been disastrous. For both of their jobs, for her innocence, and for his sanity. Better that he released his sexual tension with Alexis.

Abstinence was not a strength of his.

He stood, straightening his suit, and running a hand through his hair. Julia was probably waiting, nervously gripping a martini glass and looking for his face. She was no doubt anxious, her mind tracking down where he could be and drawing conclusions.

He stepped out of the office and was hit with a wave of cheers from down below — a large crowd swelling and building, like an anthill out of control, climbing on chairs and tables to get a better look. He followed the curve of the crowd wondering what, or who, had their attention.

He should have known better.

dangerous ground

He avoided the crowds and moved higher, stepping into a VIP alcove three stories above the dance floor to privately watch the action below—namely, Julia and Montana, and the crowd surrounding them. The bouncers were keeping the crowd under control, the girls safe, but the surge of men made him nervous. Nervous and completely fucking turned on. Their cries, cheers, raw eagerness to get to the woman that he, in some ridiculous way, thought of as his had his cock hard again almost instantly.

He unplugged the security cam to the space and stood at the edge, experiencing one heat-filled moment when Julia raised her head and their eyes connected. She smiled, a seductive gleam in her eyes that terrified him.

He had no idea who she was. This was a woman who had taken sweet, innocent Julia and dunked her into a sea of sex, allowing the liquid heat to swim through her blood, blaze through her eyes, and float from her skin like a strong perfume.

The woman on stage had no inhibitions, a smile illuminating her face, lust in her eyes as she leaned forward and pulled Montana's head to hers, her hands stealing into her hair, their kiss lengthening as the two women drew closer.

He sat, his hand moving down to adjust himself, the pulsing of his thick cock incessant, as if the fuck downstairs hadn't satisfied it. Being around her was pure intoxication, even with a hundred feet of separation between them. His eyes glued to the pair, he watched the minx who was Julia.

She pushed gently on Montana's chest, laying the girl back, her head lowering and trailing along her neck and down to the dip between her cleavage, her hands squeezing and pressing the breasts around her own face. The crowd roared, and Julia sat up, her dress fully falling down, her own bare breasts now on display for the crowd. A vibrating energy swept through the club in a physical wave.

It was too much, the crowd reaching a fever status, and he stood, reaching for his cell. Janine answered before it even completed a full ring. "Can I stop it?"

"Please," he growled. "Get them out of there."

He met them downstairs, in the girls' dressing room, naked bodies everywhere, Julia and Montana all over one another. Montana's hand trailed up Julia's leg, tugging her dress higher. He glowered at Montana, causing the girl to giggle.

"How much did they have to drink?" he asked Janine, his eyes locking with Julia. She bit her bottom lip, grinning at him, a grin that instantly turned every sensor in his body to full fledged arousal. He held her stare, willing his mind to come under control, barely listening when Janine responded.

"Five shots each — tequila."

"Get me some water," he ground out. "And have Leonard pull up the car."

He watched her sleep, her beautiful head nodding to the side as soon as the car started its forward movement. He was grateful for her sleep, grateful that those fiery eyes were closed, and he no longer had to worry about their effect on him. Her passion electrified him, frying intelligent thought patterns and making him bend to her will. And, try as he might, he couldn't get the image of her, on stage with Montana, out of his mind.

That was not the girl he knew — *thought* he knew. He didn't really know anything about her at all. She was a complete mystery, a bundle of surprises tied together with one hell of a sexy bow. Seeing her tonight, the sexuality oozing from her, her playful eroticism on display, turning on every warm-blooded man in the club … it was wreaking havoc on his already limited self-control. She had shown, in those moments, her potential. And that thought drove him absolutely crazy.

He carried her inside, pushing the door shut with his foot, and walked into the bedroom, setting her gently on the bed. Opening her suitcase, he pawed through sequins and glitter until he found a pair of worn pajama pants and a shirt. He smiled at her choice of packing, conservative over sexual. Walking back into the room, he slid the pants over her limp legs, moving briskly, trying to keep his mind in line and out of the gutter. She sat up slightly when he pulled her dress over her head, cooperating when he worked her arms into the shirt and over her head.

He said her name three times before she opened her eyes, blinking groggily at him with a slight frown on her face.

"What?" she asked, annoyed.

"I'd like you to drink some water. Do you need to go to the bathroom?"

She swallowed, her eyes on his, blinking again as she started to wake up. Then she nodded. "Yes."

He waited in the room, pouring her a glass of water and getting two aspirin. He set them on the dresser, unbuttoning his shirt and untucking it from his pants.

She stumbled in, eyeing him as she grabbed the water, gulping it down. He moved to help her, pulling back the covers and guiding her into bed. She rolled onto her back, looking up at him through heavy eyes.

"God, you are hot," she mumbled, a half smile on her lips. He grinned, pulling up the covers and reaching for the light switch. The lamp extinguished, she was in partial darkness, her beauty no less devastating in the soft, shadowy light. She freed a hand from the covers, reaching out and gripping his belt, sliding her fingers under the hem of his pants and tugging him toward her. He sat on the edge of the bed, leaning forward and brushing her hair away from her face, his eyes surveying the beautiful lines of her face.

She watched him, their eyes connecting. "You are going to be so bad for me," she whispered, her words slurring slightly. She lifted her hand, trailing it over the muscles in his chest, running it down the ridges of his stomach. "So bad," she whispered. Her eyes closed with a heavy sigh. "Tomorrow," she murmured. "Tomorrow, I'll stay away."

He leaned over, pressing his lips softly to her forehead, listening to her breath as it evened, her hand limp as it fell to the bed. Then he straightened, watching her sleep, his eyes dark.

the parting

One evening later.

Hot night around them, he stood at her front door —
weeds and dirt underfoot, the structure before him
barely habitable. She unlocked the house, taking her
bags from his hand and tossing them inside. She
leaned against the door, blocking him from any
thought of entry.

"I had fun," she said.

Fun. Like he had taken her to Dairy Queen and a
movie. He stared at her, wanting to come in,
wanting more of what he had experienced with her
in that shower — wanting her heat around his cock.

He stepped forward, her perfect face tilting up, looking into his eyes. He studied her, thinking about the weekend. Even though he had broken every rule he had set, had touched her in ways he shouldn't, he didn't regret the trip. Didn't regret accepting her advance, spending that half hour inside of her—a half hour of fucking that could destroy everything. He didn't regret the opportunity to know her, even if it was for only those brief moments in time.

I don't want a damn boyfriend. I want your cock.

Had she meant it? The next few days would be the real test. Would show how much crazy lived behind those intelligent brown eyes. He leaned down, pressed his lips gently again hers. "Goodnight."

"Night." She gave him a small wave and a tired smile and shut the door.

He watched the white door swing, heard the loose rattle as it fully shut, and wondered how long she'd wait before calling.

The porch light went out, draping him in darkness.

Brad sat at his desk, listening to the men in front of him with half an ear. This meeting was important, a strategy session for a big case, but he couldn't focus.

It was Wednesday, three days since he had dropped Julia off at her home in crack town. And no call, no email, no surprise drop-by in the East Wing.

It was a relief, having a detached conquest. He should be back-flipping happy. But it was too early for that. Three days was a good sign, but not long enough to put him in the clear. Give it a week, and then he would relax.

Eight days. Brad ground a cube of ice between his teeth, rattling the cold glass before sliding it across the counter. Eight days and no contact from Julia. It had gone from being refreshing to being annoying. Women always called. They called after he spent fifteen minutes fucking them on his desk, much less after two days drowning in limos and caviar under the Vegas skyline.

He had spelled it out in Vegas. Explained to her how he regarded sex. As entertainment, joint pleasure. How stock shouldn't be put in the act, how relationships shouldn't form just because of a sexual connection. He had told her that he couldn't be a boyfriend, couldn't be what she wanted or needed in a man.

But she should still be texting, emailing, calling, begging for more of him, especially when he had delivered more than any partner before, with both his mouth and his cock.

Instead, silence. She was doing godknowswhat with godsknowswhom and not giving him a second thought. It was maddening, made even worse by his realization that he had noticed the slight. He stood, tossing a twenty on the bar and headed home.

competition

Ten days later.

Brad stood at the conference room table, bent over, signing documents as they were presented, a flurry of pages before him.
Flip.
Sign.
Flip.
Sign.
The woman on his left notarized, the woman to her left witnessed, and the stack moved, page after page, motion after motion. He heard, through the open door, a conversation occurring in the lobby and paused, halfway through a signature.

"Naw, they finished up. Word is Broward is closing the West Wing down early, letting everyone off at five."

"About damn time. Let's go out tonight, the group of us. I'll invite Julia."

"You get a piece of that yet?"

"No, not yet. I'll run over there now and make sure she comes."

He tilted his head, listening as the pair moved on, the sounds of the office reentering his subconscious, his attention returning to the monotonous task before him, his mind turning, moving without his control in a direction he knew was dangerous.

He straightened, setting down the pen and walking to his office, shutting the door before picking up his phone. Back in the conference room, the women exchanged confused looks.

She answered quickly, a lilt in her tone, no sign of mourning or anguish in her greeting. "Julia Campbell."

"What are you doing?" He aimed for a manner that was casual, just-calling-to-chat, but the words came out rough, uncivilized. He took a deep breath, loosening his tie, and willing the anger in his body to cool.

"Just sitting here."

"With who?" He bit out the words, wanting her in front of him. Wanting to push her back on his desk and see the vigor in her eyes.

Her voice sharpened. "I assume you know or you wouldn't be calling."

Vain woman. As if he would care about her daily comings and goings. "Meaning?" he growled.

"I'm talking to Todd," she said sweetly, as if that was fucking normal, everyday business. For a brief moment, he wondered if it was.

"Let me talk to him."

"Why?" She was irritated, the emotion seeping into my voice.

"Because I need to, and he left his cell phone here."

"Just tell me the message, and I'll pass it on."

This woman would be the death of him. He growled into the phone, wanting to punish her in the only way he could think. On her hands and knees, with her sweet mouth begging him for more. *Jesus*. He was getting hard. His words came out clipped and measured. "Stop being difficult."

"I just feel like we've been here before — the only thing missing is your intimidating self darkening my doorstep."

That could be fixed. He could go four thousand square feet west and see her, tell her exactly where she could put that sassy mouth. "Just tell him to get his ass back here." He ended the call, slamming the phone down and striding to the door. He flung it open, catching the attention of the women seated before him, their dignified suits rising to see what it was he needed.

"When Todd gets back, send him in here. Immediately." He shut the door and paced to his desk, cursing every bone in that delectable woman's body.

the fight

Four hours later.

Brad ran — through the streets of downtown, weaving and ducking through three-piece suits and haggard crowds. Through neighborhoods his family controlled, streets he had been raised on, through alleys and strip malls, his legs pounding up hills, then coasting down. He breathed easily, his mind clear, peace in his eyes. He finally felt back. In control. Todd was staying away from Julia, he would stay away from Julia, and everything would return to normal. His life back in balance, work and pussy regaining their appropriate places on his score sheet. He slowed as he turned down his street, pavement turning to cobblestone, towering trees casting his body in shade, large homes set back from the street watching him as he passed. He stopped running, walking the lane of his driveway, stepping up and onto the large back porch, waving to the Mercedes as it pulled in, its confident path leading it into the garage, the doors sliding shut behind it.

He was sitting there, thirty minutes later, a tennis ball in hand, his cell phone positioned in the crook of his neck, when he heard a sound, and looked over his shoulder to see five feet eight inches of furious beauty.

Possessiveness didn't seem to go over well with Julia. Didn't make her heart fawn, pale cheeks blush, create oh-lucky-me stars in her eyes. She was pissed and spelled out her emotions clearly, despite the sway in her step and the haze over her eyes.

"You made it very clear that you didn't want a relationship. Yet *you* ran off Bob. Yet *you* told Todd to stay away from me. You are not my father, you are not my boyfriend, you are not my boss. You don't have the right to fuck with my life!"

So Todd had told her. Not that he was surprised. Based on the look she was giving him, she seemed capable of strangling the information out of a man. He stepped closer, close enough to smell her, his eyes roaming appreciatively over her skin, cataloguing every line, curve, quiver of her breath. It had been over two weeks. He had almost forgotten how incredible she was. "Do you like Todd this much? Is that what this is about?" His eyes watched her closely, very interested in her response. She couldn't like him—not that boy who skipped between offices, his innocence practically painted on like a billboard sign. Todd wasn't good enough, strong enough, or man enough for her.

"That's not the point. The point is if I *did* really like Todd, or Bob, or someone else, I don't need you walking around, scaring the hell outta people. That's not your place. It's like you don't want me, and you don't want anyone else to have me. That's bullshit, especially because you're the fucking town slut!"

"Who says I don't want you?" He stepped forward, the air quivering between them, her eyes dropping, letting him fully examine her without risk of being caught. The flutter in her neck, the swell of her lips, the flush of delicate skin. He suddenly needed to see her eyes, needed a drink of the woman he had been without. His hand forced her chin up, and their eyes met. There was a shake in hers, vulnerability, almond pools of what looked like fear. Then she blinked, and they came to life, a tiger curving through their depths and snarling at him.

She pushed at his hand. "Okay, I misspoke. It's like you don't want to date me *exclusively*. God, I forgot I was talking to an attorney and had to clarify everything."

"Let's go to dinner." He cursed the words as soon as they left his mouth. He had been free of her, and now he was digging his own grave … again. Wrestling his body into rich dirt where he would be eaten alive by scavengers.

"I already ate." Her stomach growled, and her eyes dared him to mention it.

"Then tomorrow night."

"I already have plans."

Her quick response gave him pause. Maybe it wasn't just Todd he had to worry about. He tightened his hands, balling them into fists. Fine. He had asked; she had answered. He stepped away, giving his lungs time to recharge, to recover from the erotic impact that was Julia Campbell's scent. He heard her on the phone, and looked up when she finished.

"My friend's picking me up."

He answered without thinking, his words careless, given her volatile state. "A guy or a girl friend?"

She threw her phone at him, a pathetic throw, and one he avoided easily. He laughed, her temper entertaining, and watched her eyes glitter; her body tightened with fury as she picked up the phone, then marched over to the driveway and headed back to the front of the house.

He controlled his laughter, jogging up to her, her heels skittering on the cobblestone drive, his arms catching her twice when she stumbled. She forged on, ungrateful for the saves, her focus on the front porch, which she flung her butt down on without a second glance at him.

He moved in front of her seated form, her arms tight around her legs, her face stubbornly avoiding his.

"Look, I'm sorry I said anything to Todd. That wasn't my place." The words caught in his throat, then wormed their way through his vocal cords and out of his mouth. He didn't know why he was apologizing to this woman. He should be back inside, in the cool air of his home, banging the shit out of the blonde in his bed. He wasn't sorry for speaking to Todd. She had no business going out with him. No business wasting her time on a child. And, if he could have it his way, she wouldn't waste her time with anyone but him.

"And to Bob."

"*And* to Bob. Though I didn't really say anything to Bob." No, that weakling had run out of her life with one stern glance from Brad.

She grumbled through her purse. "No, you just sucked all the air out of my office and stared him down like he was a rogue agent."

Brad sighed and sat down on the step. He wanted to take her in his arms and hold her. For no other reason than he felt like an ass and she was there. Despite his personal attraction to her, he shouldn't have spoken to Todd — should have let their possible relationship play out, and stayed on task, continued working. Then he wouldn't have opened this box, wouldn't have her at his house, a foot away, her presence invading and wiping his brain clear of rational thoughts. Reminding him of what he didn't have, and couldn't control.

She spoke again, her words taking a new direction. "And you told Todd that fraternizing with coworkers was bad business? What about fucking clients? Did you include that in your business advice? And you can't even talk about fraternizing with coworkers! Seriously, did you choke on your own bullshit?"

His jaw tightened, anger flooding through him. "Okay, Julia, you've made your point — I'm an asshole. I was out of line. I have apologized. I'm not going to sit here and have you chastise me like I'm a child. I'm not used to not getting what I want. I'm not used to being told I can't have something. I'm sorry if it pissed me off to see someone else getting you so easily." He stood up. Fuck this. Fuck this girl who made bullshit come from his mouth. Fuck her small body following him, grabbing his arm, her proximity making him hard.

"I'm not a fucking object! I'm not something that you can choose to have, or choose to toss away. Does it even matter to you what I want?"

He looked down at her hand, which gripped his bicep, wanting to remove it, to break the hold that she had on him. Then he looked at her eyes, the mere connection with them causing his breath to catch, weakness to clutch his heart and squeeze it tight.

"What is it you want?" he asked, emotions he didn't know he had coming through his voice. "What do you want from me? You want me to spend a weekend with you, have you naked against me, your smile, your laugh, and then just cut you off? Kiss you goodbye and then let anyone else have you? You want me to sit in my office and watch Todd ask you out? I'm not engineered that way. Maybe I am a territorial slut, as you put it. That might seem fucked up, but it's who I am. I take what I want, and I own what I have. I'm just trying to figure out what you want."

He despised the words leaving his mouth, hating the way they made him feel. Exposed. Open. By a girl who didn't weigh more than his cock. A girl who stared at him with intensity, who pushed buttons he didn't know he had, and had wormed her way inside a part of him that should be closed.

"I don't want a fuck buddy, much less to be owned by one." She released his arm and stepped back, heading to a jeep that idled by the curb.

He said nothing, letting her go, hoping against his heart that he would never see her again.

He strode inside, letting the door bang shut, taking the stairs two at a time. Pulling his shirt over his head as he walked through the bedroom, into the bath, he yanked open the shower door, glowering at the wet blonde who stood inside. "On the bed. Now," he ordered, jerking the band of his shorts and dropping them on the floor. "I need to fuck right now more than I need to breathe."

the problem

He fought the thought of her. Fought it the next morning as he told Todd Appleton to fuck the hell out of her if he wanted. Fought it as he pulled in each day and avoided looking at her car.

It was for the best that it hadn't gone anywhere. He needed to think of it as an interesting experiment, one he was lucky to get through unscathed. But she had gotten under his skin. Worked her sassy way under and settled in, pulling on his heart strings like a master puppeteer, whenever her easy grin and confident eyes felt like it. He needed a distraction, and selected one with strawberry blonde hair and blue eyes, bubbly and perky enough to pull his head away from Julia and put it back where it belonged. On work, on bachelorhood. On his life as he knew it, without the disruption or headache of a relationship. Because a relationship wasn't what he, his heart, or his peace of mind, needed. Fuck what he wanted.

But the blonde didn't work, his thoughts comparing every curve, every moan to Julia, and coming up short, the sex ended abruptly, his cock making the decision with which his mind still struggled. This was a serious problem, one he didn't seem to be able to fuck his way out of. Whether Julia needed it or not, *he* needed closure. He needed to know what the hell was going through her mind and what she wanted from him.

This hell needed to end. And her body, the curve of her mouth, the flash in her eyes — that seemed to be the only thing capable of bringing his life back under control.

This novella highlighted bits and pieces of Brad and Julia's initial story, told entirely from Brad's point of view. To see Julia's side of the story, and where the events in this book led, please read *Blindfolded Innocence*.

Coming Soon:
Masked Innocence: the next chapter in Brad & Julia's story
Available everywhere February 25, 2014.

The End of the Innocence, the final book in the Innocence series
Available everywhere March 25, 2014.

For a look at Masked Innocence, and other works by Alessandra Torre, please turn the page.

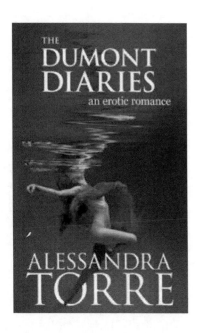

The Dumont Diaries is available as both a full-length novel, or as a four part miniseries.

Lust is a dangerous thing. It can make you believe things that are not real. It can seduce your mind and lead it blindfolded to the cliff that will be its demise.

Poor planning is what got me here. A run-down strip club ten miles outside of town, with a net worth barely over three figures. Swinging around a dented pole while truck drivers toss me greasy dollar bills.

When salvation comes in the form of drop-dead-gorgeous, complete with a limo and a thick wad of cash, my stilettos run happily out the door to freedom. Freedom with one stipulation: marriage.

So I take his offer: A life of luxury as the high-profile trophy wife of Nathan Dumont, sex and photo ops my only obligation. But sex with Nathan... is complicated. Hot, steamy, and complicated. And those days spent alone in his house? I am finding secrets. Secrets and ulterior motives that reveal my husband is holding things back. That his intentions are far from pure.

At this point, I don't know what is more in danger. My heart, my sanity, or my life.

Disclaimer: The Dumont Diaries contains a strong alpha male, super hot explicit sex, and twists and turns that might cause unnatural heart palpitations. For readers uncomfortable with public sex or a dominant male lead, please be forewarned. This book does not contain BDSM elements.

Available Now!

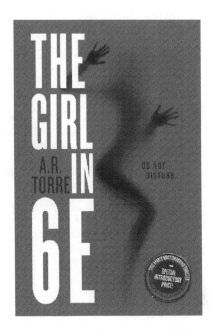

I haven't touched another human in three years. That seems like it would be a difficult task, but it's not. Not anymore, thanks to the internet.

I am, quite possibly, the most popular recluse ever. Not many shut-ins have a 200-member fan club, a bank account in the seven-figure range, and hundreds of men lining up to pay for undivided attention.

They get satisfaction, I get a distraction. Their secret desires are nothing compared to why I hide... my lust for blood, my love of death.

Taking their money is easy. Keeping all these secrets... one is bound to escape.

What if you hid yourself away because all you could think of was killing? And what if one girl's life depended on you venturing into society?

Enter a world of lies, thrills, fears, and all desires, in this original thriller from A. R. Torre.

Available Now!

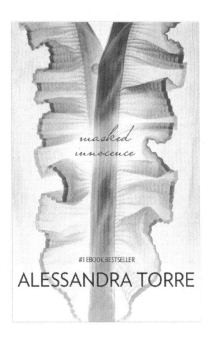

masked
innocence

ALESSANDRA TORRE

The man was sinful. It wasn't just the looks that made him dangerous, it was the cocky confidence that dominated every move, every touch. And the frustrating yet ecstatic fact about the whole package was that he could back it all up...

Julia Campbell never knows what to expect with win-at-all-costs Brad De Luca. And she's starting to like it that way. She gave up safe, conventional relationships when she let the elite divorce attorney seduce her into his world. Now that he's determined to strip her naked of every inhibition, she's in danger of falling too deep and too fast.

But their affair begins to feel even more dangerous when a murder leaves a trail of suspicion that points straight to the mob...and Brad. Trusting a man with a bad reputation and a past full of secrets seems like a mistake. But when she's forced to make a choice, the consequences will take her further than she could ever have imagined.

Available Now!

Acknowledgements & More

This book would not be possible without the support of Harlequin HQN, specifically the fabulous firecracker, who is my editor, Kate Dresser. She was kind enough to allow me to release this pre-sequel, as well as give it an editorial overview. Thanks also goes out to Madison Seidler (www.madisonseidler.com), who—as always—did a fabulous job fine-toothing this book and saving me from editorial embarrassment. And a big hug to my Twitter, Facebook, and Goodreads families--you guys have been huge in spreading the word and cultivating interest. Thank you so much for your continued interest and passion for my books.

Twitter is my crack, Facebook my midnight snack and Goodreads my IV. If you avoid social networking, you can get regular updates and information on my blog: alessandratorre.com/blog/ or sign up for my newsletter at alessandratorre.com/newsletter/

Twitter.com/ReadAlessandra
Facebook.com/AlessandraTorre0

Made in the USA
Lexington, KY
08 August 2015